Damian Harvey lives in North Wales with his lovely wife, Vicky. He has three wonderful girls, one brilliant boy and a lazy cat called Polly. He's written over 80 books for children and is busy writing more. When he isn't writing, Damian visits schools and libraries around the world to share his love of books, stories and reading. You can find out more about Damian by visiting his website: www.damianharvey.co.uk

Korky Paul was born in Blackpool and is one of seven children. He studied Fine Art at Durban Art School in South Africa and Film Animation at CalArts in California. His picture book series, Winnie the Witch, won the Children's Book Award in 1987 and has been published in over 10 languages. His other picture books include *The Dog Who Could Dig* by Jonathan Long, *The Rascally Cake* by Jeanne Willis and *The Very Noisy House* by Julie Rhodes, published by Frances Lincoln. Korky lives in Oxford with his family.

For Mila — K.P.

First published in Great Britain in 2006 and in the USA in 2007 by Frances Lincoln Children's Books
This edition published in Great Britain and in the USA in 2015 by Frances Lincoln Children's Books,
74–77 White Lion Street, London N1 9PF
www.franceslincoln.com
www.damianharvey.com

British Library Cataloguing in Publication Data available on request

ISBN 978-1-84780-712-0

Printed in China

1 3 5 7 9 8 6 4 2

www.korkypaul.com

Snail's Legs

Damian Harvey

Illustrated by Korky Paul

Frances Lincoln
Children's Books

Snail

was the fastest runner in the whole wood.

Frog

had been the fastest runner in his younger days
but he was getting old.

Frog still came to watch the races
and he would tease Snail, saying
that if he wanted to, he could still
beat him in a race. Snail loved his
old friend and didn't mind
being teased.

One day Snail and Frog were sitting on a big rock talking about races they had won when they met a man walking along the road.

"I am the King's chef," the man said, "and I am looking for an animal with very strong legs to help me prepare a special birthday treat for him. You are both such fast runners, you must have very strong legs indeed!"

The two friends were amazed. They had never met the King and now here was a chance to do something special for his birthday.

That would be a great honour indeed.

Frog puffed out his chest and replied,
"Oh yes, our legs are very strong.
But of course, mine are strongest
as I am much faster than Snail."

Snail smiled at his old friend.
After all, everybody in the wood knew
that Snail was the fastest runner.

"My old friend here is a fast runner,"
said Snail. "But as you can see, he
is very old and I am the fastest now."

"Nonsense," cried Frog.
"You will never be as fast as me."

"My dear friend," said Snail,
"you do not even race any more."

Frog knew this was true, but he could only think how grand it would be to meet the King.

"I let you win those races," Frog shouted. "A puny snail like you could never beat a grand frog like me."

Snail was furious. "Right, that does it. If you think you are fastest, we'll race right now!"

Snail jumped down from the rock and put on his running hat.

What had Frog done? He could not
beat Snail. He was much too old to race.
He would have to admit that Snail was
the fastest and had the strongest legs.

But that would mean Frog would not get to see the King.
There was only one thing he could do. He would have to race.

The runners agreed to race along the road, through the wood, over the bridge and round the pond.

The chef held up his handkerchief.

"Ready... steady...

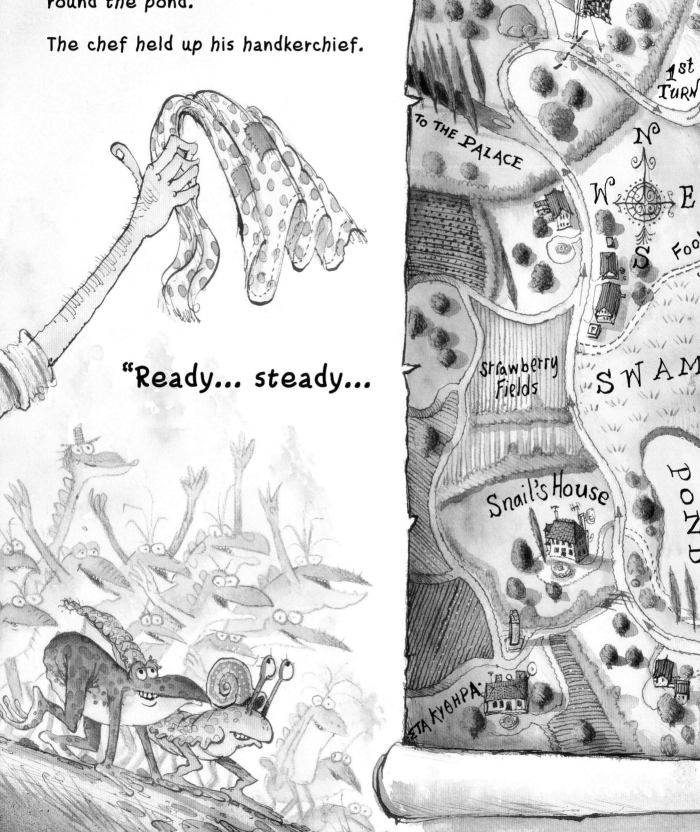

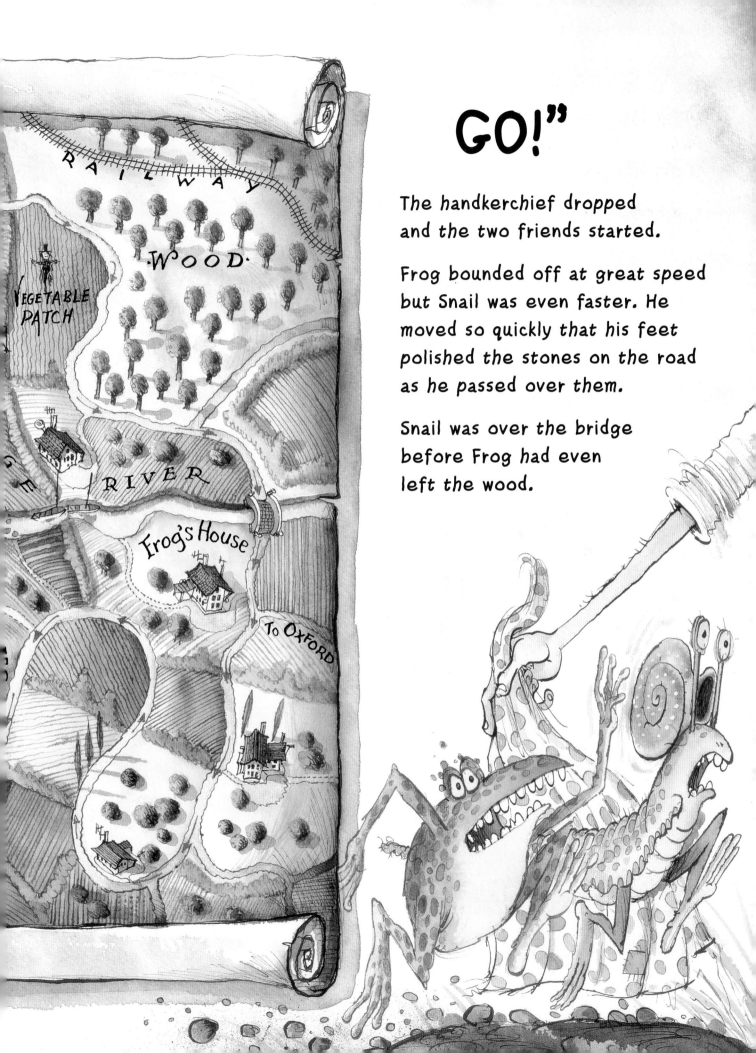

Labels on the map:
RAILWAY

WOOD

VEGETABLE PATCH

RIVER

Frog's House

To Oxford

GO!"

The handkerchief dropped and the two friends started.

Frog bounded off at great speed but Snail was even faster. He moved so quickly that his feet polished the stones on the road as he passed over them.

Snail was over the bridge before Frog had even left the wood.

As Snail ran, he passed Frog's house and remembered
all the times the two of them had sat talking and laughing.

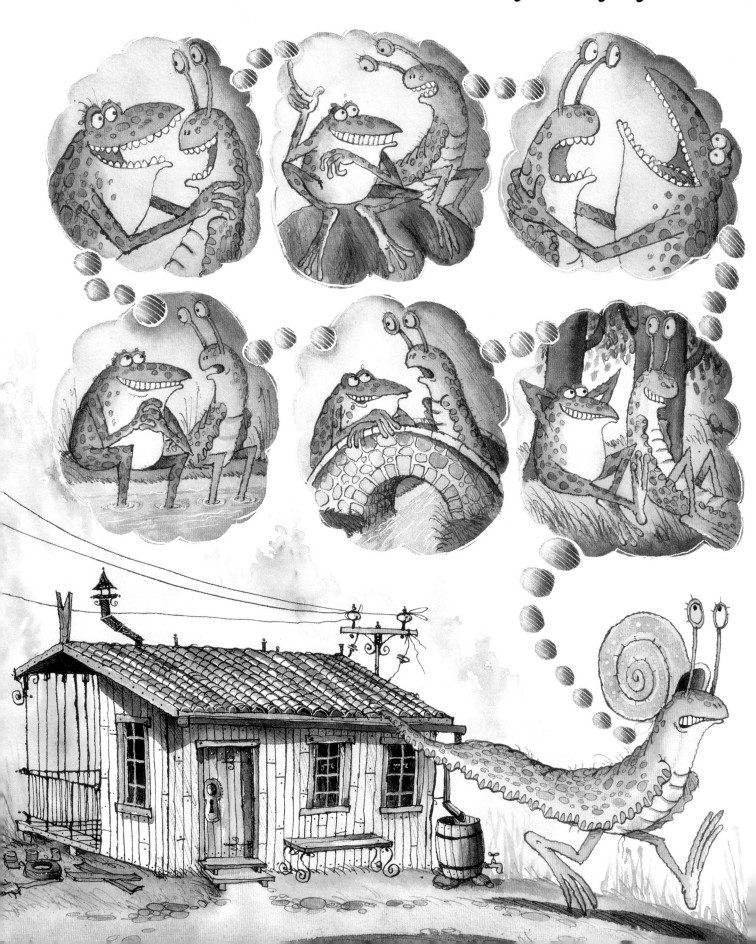

Snail stopped running and looked round.
He could see Frog coming down *the path*
from *the wood.*

He could see *the* determination on Frog's face.
Frog really did want to see the King.

Snail thought for a moment. He was only young. He had plenty of time to go and see the King. What had he been thinking, arguing with his old friend like that?

So Snail hid inside Frog's house and watched as his old friend staggered past. Frog was old and proud and Snail loved him. Frog deserved to see the King.

When Snail set off running again he went slowly, so he wouldn't catch up with Frog.

Frog had almost finished the race.
He could hardly believe it. He was going to win!
Frog could hear Snail close behind him...
but it was all over... he had won.

Frog had done it!

Snail crossed the finishing line and hugged his old friend.
"Well done! I didn't know you still had it in you!"

Frog gasped for breath and tried not to fall over.

"Well," said the chef. "It looks like Frog will be helping me with the King's birthday treat. You were very fast too," the chef told Snail. "I may come back for you another day."

The chef picked up Frog and popped him into his pocket, then headed off back to the palace.

Frog went to the palace but
never actually saw the King.

But the King did agree that
the frog's legs were very good...
very good indeed.

When word got back to the wood about what
had happened to Frog, Snail was heartbroken.
He was also frightened that the chef
would come back for him!

So Snail took to wearing
his running hat on his
back and hiding
his legs inside it.

So if you ever see a snail in *the* daytime,
it will be crawling around on its tummy
with its legs hidden away just in case
a passing chef should ever remember
how good *those* legs really are.

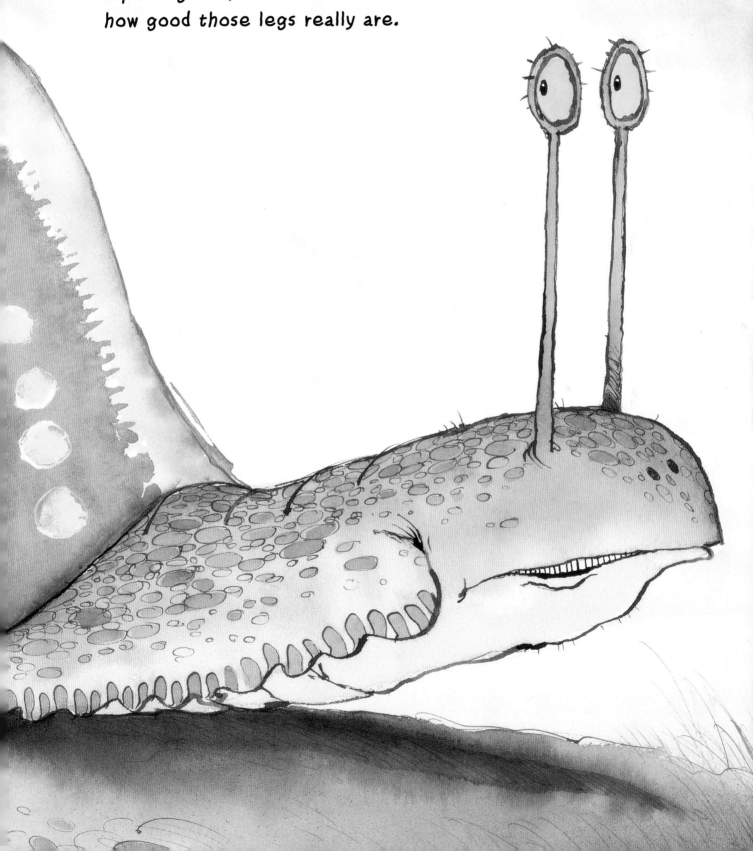

But if you go outside early
in the morning you might just see
the tiny little trails that have been
left by some of the fastest snails
as their feet polish the floor
on their moonlight runs.

MORE TITLES FROM
FRANCES LINCOLN CHILDREN'S BOOKS

The Very Noisy House
Written by Julie Rhodes
illustrated by Korky Paul

This rickety old house can be very noisy. Clomp! Clomp! Clomp! Goes the old lady's walking stick. In the room above, the dog wonders if that noise is a knock at the door – woof! Woof! Woof! And that wakes up the ginger cat in the room above who thinks the dog is chasing her – meow! Meow! Meow! Follow the riotous noises on each floor of the creaky old house as each resident makes their own crazy din.

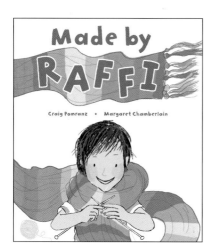

Made By Raffi
Written by Craig Pomranz
illustrated by Margaret Chamberlain

Raffi is a shy boy who doesn't like noisy games and is often teased at school. But when he gets the idea of making a scarf for his dad's birthday he is full of enthusiasm, even though the other children think it is girly to knit. Then the day draws near for the school pageant, and there is one big problem – no costume for the prince. Can Raffi save the day with his talent?

How the Library (Not the Prince) Saved Rapunzel
Written by Wendy Meddour
illustrated by Natalie Ashdown Petrie

Rapunzel sits on the sixteenth floor of an inner city block, bored, dreaming and looking out at the rain. No one can rouse her from her apathy, not the milkman or the postman or the baker or her aunt – or even the prince. But when at last a letter is delivered, it contains news that has Rapunzel on her feet again. She has a new job at the library!

Frances Lincoln titles are available from all good bookshops.
You can also buy books and find out more about your favourite titles, authors and illustrators on our website: www.franceslincoln.com